To Martin
from
The Tooth Fairy
April 14, 1993

DR. DRABBLE'S
INCREDIBLE IDENTICAL
ROBOT INNOVATION

Written by
Sigmund Brouwer and Wayne Davidson
Illustrated by
Bill Bell

VICTOR BOOKS®
A DIVISION OF SCRIPTURE PRESS PUBLICATIONS INC.
USA CANADA ENGLAND

With love,
to Kerri Lynn

ISBN: 0-89693-902-2

© 1991 SP Publications, Inc.
All rights reserved.

VICTOR BOOKS
A division of SP Publications, Inc.
Wheaton, Illinois 60187

PJ and Chelsea were on an island in the South Pacific. They had arrived there on Dr. Drabble's Brilliant All-in-One Traveling Apparatus, a machine that was part ship, part bus, and part space shuttle. PJ and Chelsea's parents were missionaries, and they traveled around the world with Dr. Drabble.

PJ wondered if having a monkey friend was very smart. PJ, you see, had a headache from hanging upside down.

"I don't want to let go!" PJ shouted to the monkey and his sister Chelsea and their pet skunk Wesley. PJ didn't know how far it was to the ground.

"You have to," Chelsea shouted. "Dr. Drabble wants us to help him." She tickled PJ.

"Aaaaagh!" PJ screamed as he let go. He fell exactly six inches. "Why didn't you tell me I was so close?"

"Because I wanted to hear you scream," his sister told him.

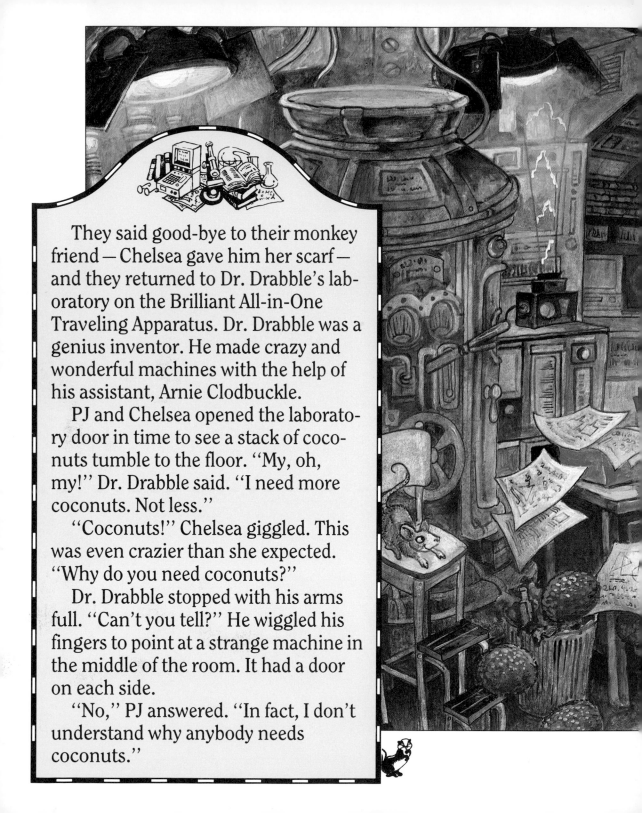

They said good-bye to their monkey friend — Chelsea gave him her scarf — and they returned to Dr. Drabble's laboratory on the Brilliant All-in-One Traveling Apparatus. Dr. Drabble was a genius inventor. He made crazy and wonderful machines with the help of his assistant, Arnie Clodbuckle.

PJ and Chelsea opened the laboratory door in time to see a stack of coconuts tumble to the floor. "My, oh, my!" Dr. Drabble said. "I need more coconuts. Not less."

"Coconuts!" Chelsea giggled. This was even crazier than she expected. "Why do you need coconuts?"

Dr. Drabble stopped with his arms full. "Can't you tell?" He wiggled his fingers to point at a strange machine in the middle of the room. It had a door on each side.

"No," PJ answered. "In fact, I don't understand why anybody needs coconuts."

"Arnie, please step into the machine," Dr. Drabble asked.

Dr. Drabble filled the top of the machine with coconuts, pulled a switch, and kicked it twice. Smoke filled the air as the machine rumbled and groaned. Pieces of coconut flew into the air. Then there was silence. Arnie Clodbuckle stepped out.

"What's so great about that?" Chelsea asked.

Another Arnie stepped out.

"I see." She giggled.

"This is the Incredible Identical Robot Innovation. One Arnie and one Incredible Identical Robot."

Dr. Drabble threw water on the robot. "See. This turns them into soap bubbles if you want, and they just float away."

"I have only one problem," he continued. "We are running short of coconuts. Would you go with Arnie to find us more?"

"Oh my," Arnie moaned when they reached the trees. "I forgot the ladder."

Suddenly a monkey chattered from behind them.

PJ and Chelsea smiled. It was their friend.

"We don't need a ladder!" PJ and Chelsea said at the same time. "He'll help us!"

Chelsea smiled sweetly. "Please, Mr. Monkey, will you help us?"

The monkey chattered happily and scampered up a tree. He began to throw down buckets and buckets of coconuts.

Arnie forgot to duck. Coconuts bounced off his head.

"Ouch!" he cried. "I'm going back to the ship!" He left them alone.

When PJ and Chelsea were finished, the monkey helped them carry coconuts back to the Brilliant All-in-One Traveling Apparatus.

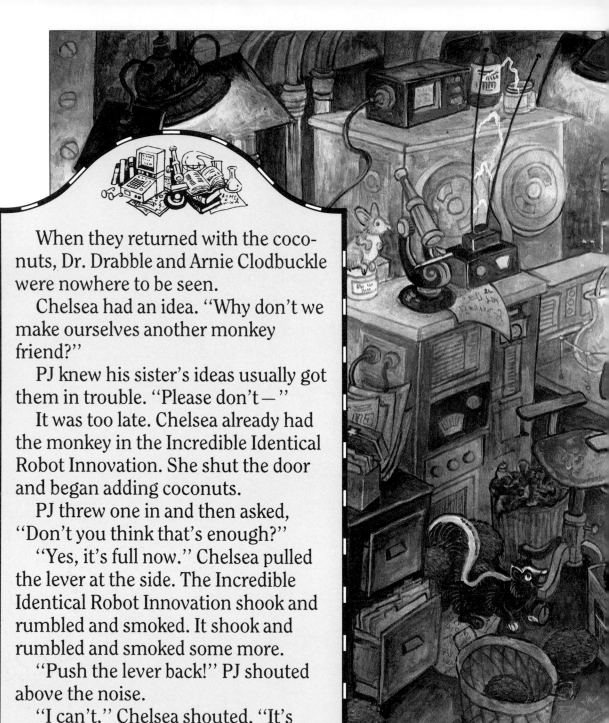

When they returned with the coconuts, Dr. Drabble and Arnie Clodbuckle were nowhere to be seen.

Chelsea had an idea. "Why don't we make ourselves another monkey friend?"

PJ knew his sister's ideas usually got them in trouble. "Please don't —"

It was too late. Chelsea already had the monkey in the Incredible Identical Robot Innovation. She shut the door and began adding coconuts.

PJ threw one in and then asked, "Don't you think that's enough?"

"Yes, it's full now." Chelsea pulled the lever at the side. The Incredible Identical Robot Innovation shook and rumbled and smoked. It shook and rumbled and smoked some more.

"Push the lever back!" PJ shouted above the noise.

"I can't," Chelsea shouted. "It's stuck."

The Incredible Identical Robot Innovation finally became quiet.

PJ's legs trembled with worry, but he managed to open the door. Their monkey friend hopped out and grinned. He enjoyed rides.

Chelsea opened the other door. Another monkey jumped out. "See. Nothing went wrong."

A second monkey hopped out. Then a third. And a fourth. Before Chelsea could shut the door, the room was filled with monkeys.

They chattered and they screeched. They stuck fingers in bottles and they spilled liquids all over. They swung from the ceiling and they swung from inventions. They pulled at levers and they pushed at buttons. They grabbed books from shelves and they kicked over the coatrack.

They even found and ate Arnie's secret chocolate chip cookie collection.

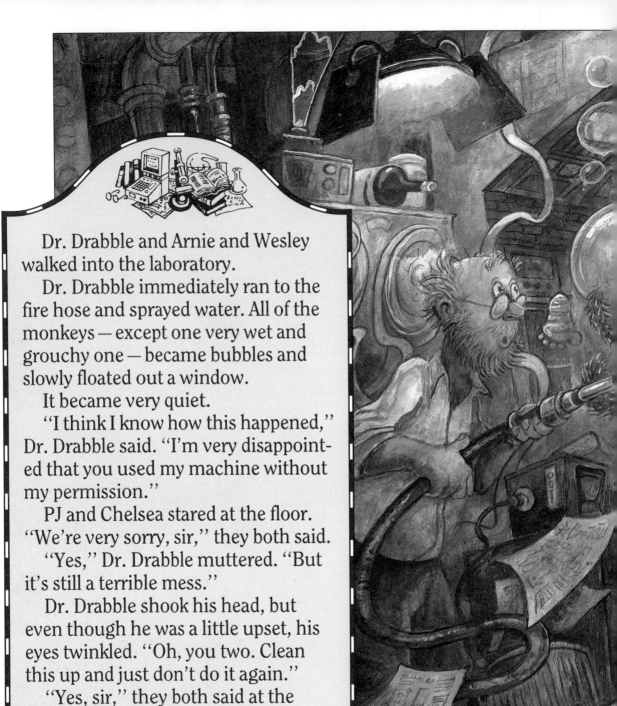

Dr. Drabble and Arnie and Wesley walked into the laboratory.

Dr. Drabble immediately ran to the fire hose and sprayed water. All of the monkeys — except one very wet and grouchy one — became bubbles and slowly floated out a window.

It became very quiet.

"I think I know how this happened," Dr. Drabble said. "I'm very disappointed that you used my machine without my permission."

PJ and Chelsea stared at the floor. "We're very sorry, sir," they both said.

"Yes," Dr. Drabble muttered. "But it's still a terrible mess."

Dr. Drabble shook his head, but even though he was a little upset, his eyes twinkled. "Oh, you two. Clean this up and just don't do it again."

"Yes, sir," they both said at the same time again.

Dr. Drabble left with Arnie.

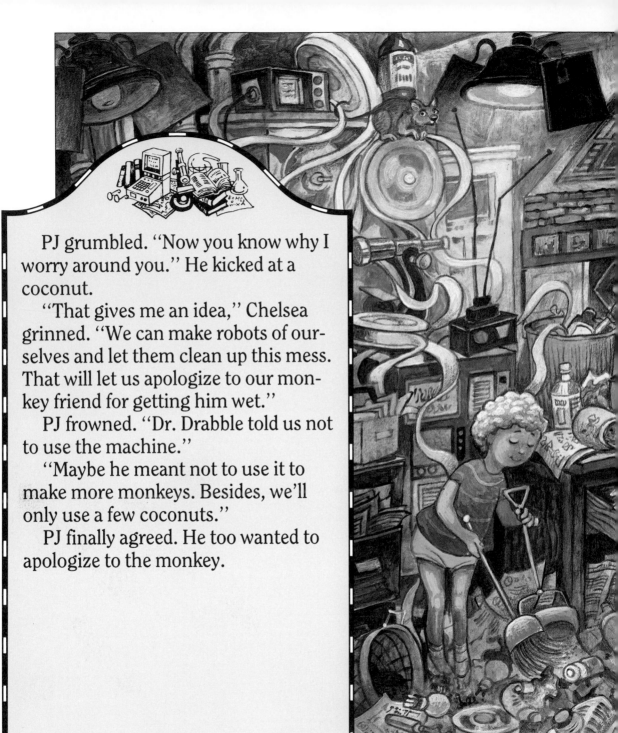

PJ grumbled. "Now you know why I worry around you." He kicked at a coconut.

"That gives me an idea," Chelsea grinned. "We can make robots of ourselves and let them clean up this mess. That will let us apologize to our monkey friend for getting him wet."

PJ frowned. "Dr. Drabble told us not to use the machine."

"Maybe he meant not to use it to make more monkeys. Besides, we'll only use a few coconuts."

PJ finally agreed. He too wanted to apologize to the monkey.

PJ and Chelsea found their monkey friend and apologized. They played for hours while their duplicates cleaned the laboratory for them.

But before the afternoon was finished, Chelsea became very quiet, and after that, even stopped playing.

Finally, she spoke. "You know, PJ. Somehow I don't feel as good as I thought I would about this."

PJ didn't say anything in return, but it was obvious by the look on his face that he felt the same way.

At suppertime, their mom said, "You both look upset. Aren't you happy about your double allowance?"

Chelsea smiled. "We're going to get a double allowance?"

Mom laughed. "Oh, Chelsea, you joker. You know full well that I gave it to you when we stopped by this afternoon with your presents."

"Presents?" PJ squeaked.

Mom laughed again. "PJ, you were quite happy with the comic books your aunt sent through the mail. How could you forget?"

Dad spoke. "Yes. Did you enjoy your gift, Chelsea?"

Chelsea's face turned sad. PJ gulped. They knew it was time to confess.

"I don't know what the present was," Chelsea said quietly. "I didn't see it."

"But we gave it to you," Mom began.

"I wish that was true," Chelsea said. "But this afternoon we pretended we were cleaning up the laboratory ourselves, when really it was someone else. And that someone else — and anything they were holding — turned into bubbles when we sprayed them with water."

PJ and Chelsea explained what they had done.

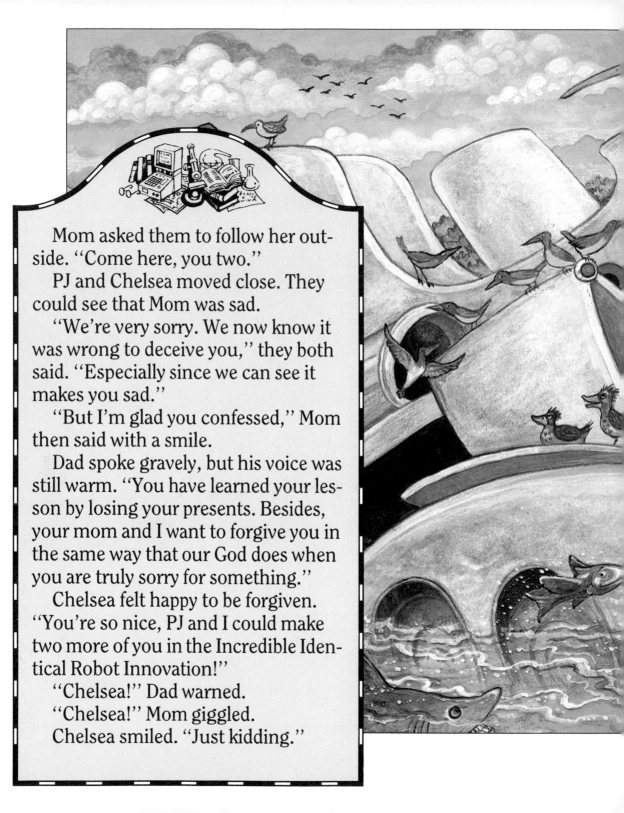

Mom asked them to follow her outside. "Come here, you two."

PJ and Chelsea moved close. They could see that Mom was sad.

"We're very sorry. We now know it was wrong to deceive you," they both said. "Especially since we can see it makes you sad."

"But I'm glad you confessed," Mom then said with a smile.

Dad spoke gravely, but his voice was still warm. "You have learned your lesson by losing your presents. Besides, your mom and I want to forgive you in the same way that our God does when you are truly sorry for something."

Chelsea felt happy to be forgiven. "You're so nice, PJ and I could make two more of you in the Incredible Identical Robot Innovation!"

"Chelsea!" Dad warned.

"Chelsea!" Mom giggled.

Chelsea smiled. "Just kidding."